The Fourth Doctor:
The Roots of Evil

BBC
DOCTOR WHO

The Fourth Doctor:
The Roots of Evil

PHILIP REEVE

PUFFIN

PUFFIN BOOKS

Published by the Penguin Group
Penguin Books Ltd, 80 Strand, London WC2R 0RL, England
Penguin Group (USA) Inc., 375 Hudson Street, New York, New York 10014, USA
Penguin Group (Canada), 90 Eglinton Avenue East, Suite 700, Toronto, Ontario, Canada M4P 2Y3
(a division of Pearson Penguin Canada Inc.)
Penguin Ireland, 25 St Stephen's Green, Dublin 2, Ireland (a division of Penguin Books Ltd)
Penguin Group (Australia), 707 Collins Street, Melbourne, Victoria 3008, Australia
(a division of Pearson Australia Group Pty Ltd)
Penguin Books India Pvt Ltd, 11 Community Centre, Panchsheel Park, New Delhi – 110 017, India
Penguin Group (NZ), 67 Apollo Drive, Rosedale, Auckland 0632, New Zealand
(a division of Pearson New Zealand Ltd)
Penguin Books (South Africa) (Pty) Ltd, Block D, Rosebank Office Park,
181 Jan Smuts Avenue, Parktown North, Gauteng 2193, South Africa
Penguin Books Ltd, Registered Offices: 80 Strand, London WC2R 0RL, England

puffinbooks.com

First published as electronic edition 2013
This edition published 2014
001

Text copyright © Philip Reeve and BBC Worldwide Limited, 2013

BBC, DOCTOR WHO (word marks, logos and devices), TARDIS, DALEKS,
CYBERMAN and K-9 (word marks and devices) are trademarks of the
British Broadcasting Corporation and are used under licence.
BBC logo © BBC, 1996
Doctor Who logo © BBC, 2014
Licensed by BBC Worldwide Limited
All rights reserved

The moral right of the author and copyright holders has been asserted

Set in Bembo MT Std
Printed in Great Britain by Clays Ltd, St Ives plc

Except in the United States of America, this book is sold subject to the condition that it
shall not, by way of trade or otherwise, be lent, re-sold, hired out, or otherwise circulated
without the publisher's prior consent in any form of binding or cover other than that in
which it is published and without a similar condition including this condition
being imposed on the subsequent purchaser

British Library Cataloguing in Publication Data
A CIP catalogue record for this book is available from the British Library

ISBN: 978-0-141-35962-5

www.greenpenguin.co.uk

MIX
Paper from
responsible sources
FSC® C018179

Penguin Books is committed to a sustainable
future for our business, our readers and our planet.
This book is made from Forest Stewardship
Council™ certified paper.

Prologue

Above the dead surface of a nameless world, far out among the Autumn Stars, the Heligan Structure hangs alone in the hard, cold light of space. A tree that has never known the tug of any gravity, except its own, it has grown immense, stretching out its massive branches in all directions. Among its glossy leaves the people build their homes and halls and galleries, but the tree does not notice them. It is sleeping, as it has slept for centuries, dreaming its long, slow, bitter dreams of vengeance . . .

I

As he walked down the steep trunk-roads, which generations of his people had bored through the living wood, Ven could hear the great tree creaking, shifting, muttering. He hated those noises. He hated the shadows that the dim bio-lamps on the ceilings cast. These deep places had always made him uneasy. But someone had to go there. Someone had to check the central trunks for canker and seek out the honey-hives and meatberry bushes, which the people needed to supplement their food supply.

Ven was fifteen now – in the first year of his manhood. Even the Justiciar's son had to take his turn among the inner branches.

Nervously he made his way along the twisting passages, shining his glow-beetle lamp into crevices, listening out for the buzzing of the small black bees that might lead him to a honey-hive. He found an out-sprouting of woody shoots that would soon block the road if they were left to grow: he marked the place with a red thread and made a note in his bark-book to report them to the pruning squads.

The creaking of the tree grew louder. It was restless tonight, Ven thought, grumbling in its sleep. And then – just when he had almost made himself believe that those noises were nothing to be frightened of – a new one reached him. A roaring, snoring sound, like some vast saw tearing at the tree: a wheezing that grew louder and louder, as if some terrible thing was rushing towards him out of the Heartwood.

Ven dropped his lamp and covered his ears with his hands. One of the lamp's precious glass panes broke and the beetles inside escaped, circling his head in a storm of dizzy little lights before scattering away into the shadows.

The noise grew louder and louder and . . . stopped.

Ven took his hands from his ears and listened. The mumblings of the great tree were all that he could hear now. They seemed quiet and comforting after that terrible new sound.

His first thought was to run back to the out-branches. But what would he say when they asked him why he'd left his work unfinished? That there had been a scary noise? He could imagine how the others would tease him about that. He was the Justiciar's son. It was his duty to show courage, and to set a good example.

So instead of hurrying away, he went towards the place where the noise had come from, around a bend of the passage and down a flight of shallow carved stairs to where a hollow space opened among a mass of vast trunks.

Ven had been to this place before. It was directly above the digestion chamber, and was used for funerals. He remembered, as a small boy, watching the shrouded body of his grandfather being lowered down through one of the dark openings in the floor to become one with the tree. The place had been empty then, nothing but the ring of mourners. Now something waited in the dim, silvery light. It was more than man-high, and a colour that Ven had seldom seen before; a rectangular thing, with windows and a door, like a small, lost room. Or a *box* . . .

Ven's mouth felt dry. *It can't be!* he thought. Not *now*, not *here*! Not appearing to *him*, after all the years of waiting . . .

Yet here it stood, solid, impossible and terrifying: the Blue Box.

2

'Leela!' shouted the Doctor. 'We're here!'

He was in one of his excitable moods. Leela threw aside the furs she slept under and went out of her cabin to find him. She had travelled through years and light-years with him, but she still didn't understand the turnings that his temper took. Sometimes he was like a child, sometimes a god. Often he seemed to be both at once.

'Come on!' he shouted, his voice echoing as he strode ahead of her somewhere through the strange, too-big spaces of the TARDIS. 'Don't you want to take a look?'

She hurried past the swimming pool, up the long spiral of a staircase and down a corridor to the control chamber. The rising-and-falling thing that told her when the TARDIS was in motion was still, so she knew that they had landed somewhere. The Doctor waited by the door, his long scarf wrapped three times around his neck, his hat pushed back on his brown mop of curls, a wide grin on his face.

'Where are we?' Leela asked.

'Surprise!' the Doctor said. 'You know you were complaining that you missed trees?'

'I did not *complain*,' said Leela. Though it was true: she was a forest-dweller, a warrior of the Sevateem. But since the Doctor had taken her from her jungle home, their travels had mostly been to treeless places: the crystalline cities of Ix, the steel hives of the Sun Makers on Pluto. Part of her longed for the dappled light of forests and the smell of growing things.

'Of course you complained!' said the Doctor. 'And you were quite right to. It reminded me that I've always meant to visit this place. It's called the Heligan Structure.'

'And there are trees here?'

'Oh, better than that! The Heligan Structure *is* a tree; one enormous, genetically engineered tree, the size of a small moon. Earth people in the twenty-fourth century use these things to help terraform alien worlds.'

'Terror . . . what?'

'Terraform: to make Earth-like. I've seen whole forests of Heligans hanging high in the upper atmospheres of planets in the Cygnus Sector, slowly breathing in carbon dioxide, breathing out oxygen. The leaves act as solar collectors. This one's different though: much bigger, and all alone.'

He put a picture of it on the TARDIS's screen for her. It did look like a moon, she thought. A moon of spiky green leaves, with spires and windows and covered balconies and jutting pointy bits poking out all over it. It was floating above a world that looked as lifeless as a cinder.

'It doesn't look like a tree . . .'

'No,' agreed the Doctor. 'More like a giant Christmas decoration built by squirrels. The tree's inside: root ball in the centre, trunks and branches radiating out in all directions. And people live on it! There's no life on the planet below, but here they are, hundreds of them, living in this tree. A whole city of tree houses, slowly linked together over hundreds of years. It's a space station, Leela. A wooden space station!'

Leela stared at the thing. 'Why would people want to live there?'

'Do you know, I have absolutely no idea!' said the Doctor, his grin growing wider, as it always did when he arrived in some new place. 'Let's find out!'

He unlatched the door. Leela checked she had

her knife, and looked round for K-9. The robot dog was parked under the main console. Multicoloured wires trailed from one of his hatches to a port on the console's underside. He was motionless, his single eye unlit, but when Leela called his name he raised his head and the antennae on top swivelled towards her.

'Recharging batteries, mistress,' he said. 'Estimated time remaining: two hours, thirty-seven minutes, fourteen seconds . . .'

'All right, K-9,' said the Doctor. 'You wait here. There's a good dog.'

'Affirmative, master.'

'But, Doctor!' Leela protested. 'What if we are attacked? The little metal one fights well!'

'I don't need K-9 to look after me,' the Doctor assured her. 'I'm sure there'll be no danger here anyway.'

He might be sure, but Leela was not. She could never understand why the Doctor was so careless of danger. It was a good thing he had her to look after him, she thought, as he opened the TARDIS door and they stepped out together into dim, green light and the earthy, warm-compost smell inside the great tree.

The TARDIS had materialised in a sort of woody cave, its walls formed by thick trunks, which had twined and fused together over centuries. The floor was a latticework of roots. Here and there a dark hole opened between them. The Doctor bounded around this space delightedly, running his hands over the smooth silver bark, saying things like: 'Grown from heavily modified holly DNA, I think!' and 'Too small to create this much gravity on its own . . . They must have a generator somewhere. That's how they stop the atmosphere escaping into space . . .'

Leela ignored him. He might know about DNA and gravity and space, but she knew trees. She'd known each individual tree within a day's walk of her home village. Even as a child she'd understood that trees each had their own character, like people. She looked around her at the scarred and knotted trunks, and listened to the way that this tree creaked and stirred and shifted. It seemed to her that it was ancient – and evil.

And she could feel eyes on her. Someone was watching them. She turned, reaching for her knife. A narrow passageway opened between the trunks nearby, and from the darkness there a boy stared out: wide, scared eyes in a brown face.

'Doctor . . .' she whispered.

The Doctor saw the boy. 'Hello!' he said.

The boy seemed unable to move, unable to speak. He cowered a little deeper into the shadows as the Doctor walked towards him, but that was all.

The Doctor looked pleased to see the boy. He always looked pleased to see everybody. He reached into his pocket and pulled out a crumpled paper bag. 'Would you like a jelly baby?' he asked, holding it out to the boy.

The boy looked down at the bag, then up again at the Doctor's reassuring grin. He didn't look at all reassured. He said, 'You are really him! You are *the Doctor*!'

'That's right. And this is Leela. What's your name?'

'Ven,' said the boy.

'Ven? That's a good name. Catchy. Easy to remember.'

The boy said, 'It's short for "Vengeance-Will-Be-Ours-When-The-Doctor-Dies-A-Thousand-Agonising-Deaths".'

The Doctor's grin faded. 'Well,' he said, 'that *is* a bit of a mouthful. I can see why you shortened it . . . Are you *sure* you wouldn't like a jelly baby?'

A tremor rippled through the tree, making all the trunks and branches creak and whisper, shuddering the roots underfoot.

'There is danger here,' said Leela firmly. She

turned back towards the TARDIS. But in the few seconds that her attention had been focused on the Doctor and Ven, the chamber had changed. New shoots were sprouting silently from the floor and twining around the TARDIS, enclosing it in a cage of living wood, which grew thicker with each passing instant. Leela ran forward and tugged at a shoot. It was young, green and pliable, but as fast as she pulled it away from the TARDIS another grew to take its place.

'Do something!' she shouted at the Doctor. 'Use your magic!'

'The sonic screwdriver, you mean?' The Doctor took off his hat and scratched his head, staring at the mass of branches and tendrils where the TARDIS had been. 'It has no effect on wood, I'm afraid.'

Leela gave a cry of frustration and drew her knife. The thinner tendrils parted easily enough, amid sticky splatterings of sap, but more were sprouting all the time. The ones that had grown first were already thick and woody.

'You will never free it!' shouted Ven. Outraged by what Leela was doing to the tree, he forgot his fear of the Doctor and ran to her, struggling to pull her away. 'The tree has awoken! You will never get your box back! You will die here! Let justice be done!'

Leela wrenched free of him and spun round, cursing, ready to drive her knife through him despite the Doctor's shout of 'No!' But before she could strike, another tremor shook the tree, far worse than the first. Caught off-balance, she pitched forward, and would have fallen had the Doctor not caught her. Ven was not so lucky; stumbling backwards, he slipped into one of the ominous dark openings in the floor and vanished with a terrified scream.

As the shaking ceased, the Doctor and Leela ran to the edge of the hole. It opened into a shaft, smooth-walled and sticky with sap. Far below they could see a greenish glow. It seemed to Leela that they were looking down into a lake of thick green fluid. The composty smell came strongly up the shaft, and so did the whimperings of Ven, who was clinging to some tiny handhold halfway down.

'Don't worry!' called the Doctor. 'We'll soon have you out of there!'

Leela could not see why they should help him – he was their enemy! He had attacked them! – but she wanted to please the Doctor, so instead of arguing she leaned into the shaft, stretching down both hands towards the terrified boy.

He was far beyond her reach. The Doctor pulled her out again. 'No, no, no . . . We don't want you falling in after him.' He peered down at Ven again. 'What's down there?' he called. 'Is there any way out at the bottom?'

The boy shook his head.

'Doctor!' said Leela, tugging at his sleeve. 'There

are forest plants at home that trap small creatures and dissolve them in pools of slime among their leaves. This tree must be the same, but bigger!'

The Doctor looked at her, his eyes very wide, his expression deadly serious. 'Heligans aren't usually carnivorous. I suppose this one is just too big to sustain itself on sunlight alone. Someone has been monkeying about with its DNA sequences . . . That must be the digestion chamber down there. I expect they shovel all their waste into it. Their dead too. Making the tree stronger. Very efficient . . .'

'Doctor, what about the boy?'

'Eh? Oh yes . . .' He peered down the shaft again. Ven was still clinging there. 'How far down do you think he is?' the Doctor asked. 'I'd say about twenty feet; that's about six metres, or roughly . . . let me see . . . two and a half Rigellian floons . . . Yes, this should do it . . .'

As he spoke, he was unwinding the long, stripy scarf from around his neck. He tied one end firmly around a protruding root at the mouth of the shaft and lowered the other carefully down towards the boy.

'Catch hold of this, Ven!'

The boy looked as if he'd been asked to touch a poisonous snake. Perhaps he thought it *was* a poisonous snake, it occurred to Leela. 'It will not hurt you,' she promised. 'It is called a "scarf". It is like a cloak, only pointless. Take it! He is trying to save your life!'

The boy still looked just as scared. 'But the B-Blue Box,' he stammered. 'And he said . . . He's the *Doctor*!'

'Now catch hold,' said the Doctor cheerfully. 'There's a good chap.'

For a moment Ven just hung there, staring up. Then, with a yelp of fear, he let go of his precarious handhold and snatched hold of the scarf. He dangled for a moment, flailing for a foothold on the shaft walls. Little flakes of bark, dislodged by his boots, went tumbling down to splash into that green lake below.

'I hope he doesn't stretch it,' the Doctor whispered to Leela, as they watched him scramble towards them. 'Still, that's one problem solved. Now to think about untangling the TARDIS . . . There's always a solution to these little emergencies. You just have to think sideways at them.'

Leaving Leela to keep an eye on the boy while he climbed back up, the Doctor rolled over on to his back and clasped his hands behind his head. He always thought best when he was relaxing. But just as he was about to turn his mind to the problem of the TARDIS, he noticed that he and Leela were no longer alone. While they had been busy rescuing young Ven, three men and a girl had crept silently into the chamber behind them. All four wore what appeared to be wooden armour, and all carried spears. The girl, who seemed to be their leader, was pointing hers at the Doctor's throat.

The Doctor beamed at her. 'Hello! I think you'll get on rather well with my friend Leela here.'

Leela glanced round, saw the newcomers, and sprang up, reaching for her knife. The Doctor gestured at her to keep it in its sheath. If his young companion had a fault, he thought, it was this habit of hers of trying to stick knives in people as soon as she met them. Personally, he much preferred to get them chatting. People were generally much less inclined to want to kill you once you'd chatted for a bit, and if they weren't, well, at least you could use the time to think of an escape plan . . .

He touched a curious finger to the tip of the spear that the girl had levelled at him. 'Ouch! Wooden, isn't it? It seems very sharp.'

'It is,' said the girl, who didn't appear to want to chat. 'You'll find out just *how* sharp unless you tell me who you are and what you're doing here.'

'Oh, we were just passing, you know,' said the Doctor, smiling brightly. 'Thought we'd look in. I'm the Doctor.'

The girl glared. The men behind her looked terrified. One said, 'It *is* him!' Another warned, 'Be careful, Aggie! Remember, "The Doctor is a Master of Deceit".'

'Aggie?' said the Doctor thoughtfully. 'I wonder what that's short for?'

The girl's nostrils flared proudly. 'My *full* name is Agony-Without-End-Shall-Be-The-Doctor's-Punishment.'

'Ah,' said the Doctor. 'You know, Leela, just between ourselves, I'm starting to feel that I'm not entirely welcome here.'

'Chairman Ratisbon felt the tree wake, and sent me to find out what roused it,' said the girl.

'Chairman Ratisbon, eh?'

'You have heard of him?'

'No. Who is he?'

'He is the one who has been chosen to be the instrument of our people's vengeance,' said Aggie proudly.

'Well, good for him . . .'

'Watch out!'

It was one of the spearmen, pointing to the mouth of the shaft.

Ven was so dishevelled and smeared with sap that they did not recognise him at first as he came scrambling up, gasping with the effort of the climb. Then Aggie cried, 'Ven!'

'He is the Doctor!' said Ven, pointing. 'He arrived in the Blue Box, just as the legends tell, and the great tree awoke and captured it to stop him from escaping.'

'The great tree be praised!' said Aggie.

'But . . . He saved my life!' Ven untied the scarf and handed it back to the Doctor. 'I would have fallen into the digestion chamber, but he risked his

scarf to save me . . . So can he really be the Doctor?
The Doctor would not have done that, would he?
And he looks unlike the carving.'

'Perhaps he has disguised himself,' said Aggie.
'Perhaps he saved you for some purpose of his own.'
She looked at the Doctor again. 'The day we have
waited for so long has come at last. We must take
him to Chairman Ratisbon.'

'No,' said Ven. 'It is the Justiciar who leads us,
not Chairman Ratisbon. You must take the Doctor
to the Justiciar. She will decide.'

'And because you are her son, do you think that
gives you the right to command the Chairman's
guards?' asked Aggie.

'No, but . . . It is the ancient law: when the
Doctor comes, the Justiciar will try him before all
the people.'

Aggie nodded haughtily. 'Very well. We shall
take him before the Justiciar, and send word to
Ratisbon to prepare the Chair.' She beckoned one

of her men over. 'Stay here; guard the Blue Box. The rest of you, bring the prisoners.'

An odd splashing sound came from down below; a strange, wet rustling from deep in the digestion chamber. 'What was that?' asked the Doctor, as Aggie's spearmen dragged him to his feet. 'Did anybody else hear that?'

Nobody was listening to him, except Leela. She knew what the noises meant. *The tree is angry*, she thought, but she didn't say so. He would only tell her that she was being unscientific.

Below them, unseen, something was happening in the complex of woody caves that formed the giant Heligan's digestion chamber. Dark growths studded the walls and roof down there. They had been no bigger than footballs until now, but they were starting to swell, bigger and bigger, thorny spines pushing through their outer skin. Already a few were so large that their own weight tugged them free of the sockets they had grown in. They rolled down into the lake of green broth and bobbed there for a few moments like floating mines. Then, unfolding, putting out roots and feelers, they began to drag their way ashore . . .

3

Leela was uncertain just how far they travelled through the endless windings and twistings of the Heligan Structure. Gradually the passageways through which their captors drove them began to be walled with planks and panels rather than simply hollowed through living wood, and finally they entered the tree-house city in the out-branches. Once or twice they crossed broad thoroughfares, and passed openings that gave glimpses into great chambers where food was being prepared, and bark-fibres turned into cloth. Sometimes they went through busy spaces where people came crowding round to watch the strangers led past. Leela heard the news passing from mouth to mouth, crackling like a brush-fire: 'It is the Doctor! The *Doctor*!' People shouted it in the wooden arcades, spreading the news to distant branches. But Aggie and her companions would not stop, just jabbed the prisoners with their wooden spears and forced them onwards.

'They're not very hospitable,' the Doctor whispered. 'But you can't help admiring them. They've built this whole world out of Heligan wood. Remarkable!'

Leela thought what was really remarkable was the way he could remain so light-hearted while they were being led to whatever awful fate these tree people had planned for them. He had that grin again. She supposed it was because he had lived so long and seen so many wonders. It must grow boring after a while. Anything new delighted him.

'I suppose your ancestors were stranded here?' he asked, looking back at Aggie and the spearmen. They would not answer him, so he tried calling out to Ven, who was still trailing behind. 'Space-wreck, was it? And you salvaged just one Heligan and managed to turn it into a sort of living space station . . . Ingenious! How long have you been here?'

'The great tree has been the home of our people for nine hundred years,' said Ven. 'Yes, our ancestors were trapped here . . .'

'But there was no wreck,' said Aggie fiercely. 'It was *you* who stranded us, Doctor.'

'Really? Me? No, I think there's been a bit of a misunderstanding . . .' the Doctor began, but the conversation was at an end, and so was the journey. One of the spearmen opened a carved door, and Aggie shoved the Doctor and Leela through it into a big octagonal room with carved panelled walls. That side of the Heligan Structure was turned towards the sun, and leaf-dappled sunlight came dancing through a window made from a single translucent sheet of cellulose. A woman waited for them there; handsome, grey-haired, the hem of her tea-coloured bark-fibre robes brushing the floor as she rose from her seat and came forward to study the Doctor.

Aggie and her men forced him to his knees.

'Mother,' said Ven. 'It is him!'

The woman frowned. 'He is not like the carving.'

'I saw the Blue Box,' said Ven. 'But . . .'

'He admitted himself that he is the Doctor,' said Aggie. 'I shall fetch the Chairman. Justice shall be done.'

'So you must be the Justiciar?' said the Doctor, smiling up at the woman as Aggie left. He pointed at the chair that she had risen from; a thing of plastic and metal, quite unlike the rest of this wooden world. 'That's the pilot's chair from a Wyndham-class starship, isn't it? An antique, by the look of it . . .'

'We have waited a long time for you, Doctor . . .'

The Justiciar's voice was stern, but she looked troubled. All her life she had known of the Doctor. She remembered as a little girl being told by her grandmother, 'Be good, or the Doctor will come and get you!' But she had never really believed in him. A man who travelled through space and time in a blue box? It sounded so unlikely! She had thought he was just a symbol; a useful myth that the founders had invented to bind the people together and help them to survive in this strange place. When she was elected Justiciar she had sworn solemnly that she was ready to sit in judgement on the Doctor if he should return – but a hundred Justiciars before her had sworn that same oath, and he never had. She had never imagined that it would fall to her to deliver sentence on him.

'For nine centuries our people have awaited their revenge,' she said, looking into his wide, intent eyes, and wondering still if it was really him. 'Their glorious leader, Director Sprawn, promised our forefathers that you would come one day, Doctor. He designed the Heligan Structure to lure you. An intergalactic nosy parker like the Doctor will not be able to resist such a thing, he told them. And here you are.'

'Now what is all this about vengeance?' The Doctor started to rise, but the spearmen forced him down again. 'Vengeance for what? I've never done anything to you!'

'Perhaps you have betrayed so many people that you have forgotten us,' said the Justiciar.

'The Doctor would never betray anyone!' said Leela angrily.

'Hush, Leela . . .'

'Nine hundred years ago,' the Justiciar went on, 'our forefathers were colonising a world called Golrandonvar. They were from Earth. Their forest of Heligan trees was transforming the atmosphere; mining and construction operations were under way. And then you arrived in your blue box . . .'

'Golrandonvar?' asked the Doctor. 'No, it doesn't ring a bell, I'm afraid. But then I've visited such a lot of places . . . Did it look a bit like a gravel pit? You'd be amazed how many alien worlds look just like gravel pits . . .'

'Mother,' said Ven. 'He saved my life. I would have fallen into the digestion chambers if it had not been for him. Why would the Doctor do such a thing?'

'Because he is a good man!' said Leela. 'That is why he saved you! That is why he stopped me killing the angry girl and these curs with their toy spears! He would never let anyone be harmed who did not deserve it!'

The Justiciar looked at her.

'I believe you are telling the truth,' she said. 'I believe you truly think he is good. But perhaps he has deceived you. Our people have a saying: "The Doctor is a Master of Deceit: even his smiles are stratagems." He *seemed* friendly enough when he arrived on Golrandonvar nine centuries ago. But then he sided with the natives of the planet; vicious, primitive, swamp-dwelling creatures called the Thara. He helped them to rise up against our ancestors, and drive them from that promising world. One ship, that was all he left them, and just enough fuel to make it to this rock we orbit now. That is why, for all these years, we have awaited the Doctor's return. So that he can be made to pay for what he did to us.'

'Yet he did save my life,' Ven said.

'And I am grateful,' acknowledged the Justiciar. 'It shall be taken into account at his trial.'

The door crashed open again. Aggie stood there. Beside her was a tall old man, gaunt and fierce-eyed, his white brows bushy as an eagle owl's. There were more people behind him; people with spears and clubs, peering nervously over one another's shoulders for a glimpse of the Doctor.

'There will be no trial!' the old man boomed – his voice was nearly as rich and deep as the Doctor's own. 'None of your so-called justice for the Doctor, Justiciar! Have you not felt the tree-quakes? The Heligan is awake! It knows the Doctor is here, and it does not want justice. It wants revenge!'

4

Down in the Heligan's rooty heart, the man who had been left behind to guard the TARDIS was growing bored. He walked all the way round that thicket of new trunks, peeking in through the gaps between them, but he could barely make out the Blue Box, and from the bits he could see it did not look nearly as scary or impressive as the old stories made it sound. It was supposed to be 'bigger on the inside', whatever that meant, but he could not see in through the windows.

Small noises came constantly now up the shafts in the floor: splashings and slitherings and strange, scratchy rustlings. He ignored them. The old tree was restless tonight, and who could blame it? It was trembling and shaking itself, full of new sounds.

Deep in thought, and studying the TARDIS, he did not notice the things that came squeezing out of the shafts all around him. As spiky as conker casings, as tall as men, they moved like crabs on their crab-leg roots, slow at first, then scuttling suddenly . . .

The tree was restless tonight.

No one heard his screams.

'Revenge?' asked the Justiciar, turning from her prisoners to confront the angry newcomer who had interrupted her. 'Yes, but it must be done honourably, Chairman. I am the Justiciar, and I say that we must have a trial. We must make certain that this really is the Doctor; he should be allowed to have his say before you put him to death.'

'You are not fit to be Justiciar!' sneered Chairman Ratisbon. 'You are like so many others nowadays; you think the Doctor is only a fairy-tale monster to scare our naughty children with.'

The Justiciar blushed angrily. 'Hasn't everyone wondered that? Everyone with any intelligence? Even fierce old men like you, Cut-Out-The-Doctor's-Living-Heart Ratisbon? But here he is, and he says that he is the Doctor, and by our ancient laws he must face judgement.'

'There is no need,' said Ratisbon. 'Judgement was passed on this traitor nine hundred years ago. The sentence is agony and death, and it is my duty to see that it is carried out. Take him to the Chair!'

And although the Justiciar held up her hands and commanded them to stop, there was no stopping the men who poured into her chamber, who seized hold of the Doctor and dragged him roughly away. Leela, while her own guards were distracted, snatched back the knife that one had taken from her and ran to rescue him, but one of Ratisbon's men felled her with a blow from a spear-butt. She landed on all fours, groggy, blood dripping from a cut on her forehead. Ven ran to her, and his mother came and knelt beside her, dabbing at the wound with a cloth.

'Leave me alone! It is barely a scratch . . .' Leela tried to fling them away, to run after the Doctor. They held her back. 'Where are they taking him?' she demanded. 'I thought you were leader here?'

The Justiciar said, 'I thought so too, but it seems not. Ratisbon is our executioner. It seems he is impatient to get to work.'

The room quivered. The whole tree seemed to be stirring restlessly, like some great animal troubled in its dreams. From outside the room came a rustling sound, like someone dragging a heavy bundle of twigs.

One of the men who had been lingering in the open doorway, not sure whether to stay with the

Justiciar or follow Chairman Ratisbon, suddenly shouted out in fear. 'Justiciar!'

He stumbled back into the room and tried to shut the door, but something shoved it violently open. The rustling sound was very loud, and the room was suddenly filled with the compost smell that Leela remembered from down below. She looked at Ven and his mother, saw fear and incomprehension on their faces, and stood up, knife in hand, ready to meet this new peril face to face . . .

Except it had no face. A hard greenish shell studded with sharp spines, a cluster of busy, scuttling, claw-like roots, delicate tendrils that groped and fluttered, a thick hairy stem, but nothing anywhere that looked like eyes or a mouth.

Behind her one of the Justiciar's women shrieked, and the creature swung towards the sound. *It's blind*, thought Leela, *but it is not deaf* . . . She motioned to the others to be quiet. She did not know if she could fight this thing – not alone. A few of the men in the room had spears, but they looked too scared to use them. Anyway, where did you stab a thing like that? What would its weak points be?

Someone whimpered. The thing twitched, creeping forward on its skirt of roots, tendrils reaching out to feel the air ahead. Leela held her breath, trying not to tremble as a tendril-tip came within a hand's breadth of her face.

Then, from somewhere outside, there was another scream – *There must be more of them*, thought Leela – and the creature whirled around and scuttled out. More screams in the corridor; whispers from the huddled, frightened people in the room.

'What was that?' hissed Leela.

'I don't know!' Ven whispered back. 'I've never seen anything like it.'

'The Doctor,' she said. 'He will know what they are, what to do.'

'But Ratisbon has the Doctor!' said the Justiciar.

'Then we must save him!'

The Justiciar looked at her for a moment, then slowly nodded. To the people in the room she said, 'You who have weapons, come with me; the rest, gather at the Hall of Justice. Be careful of those . . . those whatever-they-ares.'

Leela was already at the door. She acted as if she had forgotten that she had ever been their prisoner, and they did not try to remind her. Outside, the wooden corridors were filled with the rooty rustling and wet vegetable smell of the creeping things. Leela gripped her knife more firmly.

'Where have they taken him?' she asked.

5

They had taken him down stairs, and through carved and polished wooden corridors, until at last they came to a heavy door. Chairman Ratisbon himself unlocked it and flung it wide. And there, in a big, shadowy chamber, stood the Chair.

The Chair was Ratisbon's own invention. For many years the executioner had sensed that belief in the Doctor was fading and the hunger for revenge growing weak. He had set out to remind his people of their old hatred, and show his own faith in the ancient legends, by preparing the device on which the Doctor would be tortured and killed when he finally showed up. Over the years he and his supporters had gathered wood and much of the remaining metal from the original colonists' dismantled starship, and they had built the Chair.

It was a metal and plastic chair much like the Justiciar's throne, but it was surrounded by a spiky halo of sharp implements mounted on articulated wooden arms. There were drills and blades and needles, syringes filled with the tree's own acids, rubber tubes and electric terminals, ingenious devices designed to peel and carve and crush.

'Did you think death would be quick, Doctor?' sneered Ratisbon. He gestured to the Chair. 'Please – take a seat.'

'Oh, that's all right,' said the Doctor. 'I'd rather stand, if it's all the same to you.'

The chamber lurched; the walls creaked. Some of the people who had gathered there cried out in fear, and from outside came noises; shouts and screams, the crash of something falling.

Ratisbon sniffed irritably. 'What now?'

The door opened. Aggie burst in, shouting, 'Chairman! There are . . . things! They are coming up out of the Heartwood! They are everywhere!'

More shouts behind her, then a strange noise, like someone dragging a big bundle of sticks. Ratisbon flapped his hands, waving the annoyance away. 'Then deal with it, Agony-Without-End. I daresay it is just some trick by the Justiciar. She hasn't the stomach to let real justice be done . . .'

But even as he spoke, the floor behind him bulged and split, its ancient planking splintering upwards as a great blow struck it from beneath. The Chairman's followers scattered as something large and spiny squeezed up into the chamber. Others were rising too, all around the room. They reached out tendrils to seize struggling and screaming men. One snatched Ratisbon, wrapping roots around him, dragging him backwards towards the hole it had emerged from.

The Doctor, forgotten by his frightened guards, ran to the Chair and broke off the arm that held the biggest, sharpest blade. By the time he turned back, Ratisbon was vanishing through the floor. The Doctor ran to him, slashing at the roots that held him. He grabbed one of the Chairman's flailing hands and shouted, 'Hold on, man!' and 'Aggie, help!' But Aggie was battling against another of the creatures. Roots wrapped around Ratisbon's throat and tightened, squeezing and crushing. His fingers slipped limply from the Doctor's grasp; the thing dragged his body down into the darkness under the floor.

The Doctor ran to help Aggie. Defending herself with her spear, the girl was managing to hold at bay the monster that was attacking her. When the Doctor joined her it retreated, waving its roots and tendrils threateningly, making fierce rustling noises, which sounded like wind in treetops.

'Come on!' the Doctor shouted. He and the other survivors fled from the chamber, and Aggie slammed the door behind them. The corridors outside were full of rustlings too, and shouts and shrieks, which told them that more of the creatures were loose all through the maze of the Heligan Structure.

'What are they?' asked Aggie.

'I should say they are some kind of mobile spore,' said the Doctor. 'That's how Heligans reproduce, normally. They should be setting off on their own to turn into new trees. But they've been altered, re-programmed if you like. Turned into warriors . . .'

Aggie nodded slowly, stupid with shock. 'The tales tell how when the Doctor comes, the tree itself will defend us from him. But why would its warriors attack *us*? We too are the tree's own children!'

'Well, I should imagine it's me they're after,' said the Doctor. 'That's the trouble with plants – they aren't always very bright. I expect we all look the same to them. They just grab anything that makes a sound . . .'

'Kill him, Agony-Without-End!' shouted one of the men nearby. 'He is in league with the monsters!'

'No!' said Aggie angrily. 'He helped me. He fought bravely, and tried to save the Chairman.'

The door behind them creaked, bowing outwards under the force of some heavy weight. They could hear the root-tips of the angry spores scrabbling against it. From the other direction more noises came – quick, furtive scufflings. Shadows moved where the corridor twisted. Aggie gripped her spear.

'No . . .' said the Doctor.

Around the turn of the passage came, not a spore-warrior, but another group of frightened human beings. Among them the Justiciar, Ven and Leela, who ran to the Doctor and hugged him tight. 'I knew you would escape! I came to save you! There are things, creatures . . .'

'We know, we know,' he said.

'They are everywhere!' said Ven.

'We must make our way to the Hall of Justice,' said the Justiciar. 'That is where our people gather in times of danger. Together, perhaps we can hold them off.'

She pointed down a broad corridor. They ran along it, pausing once in the shadows at an intersection while a cluster of spores went rustling by. When they reached the big double doors, Ven and one of the men heaved them open.

The spores did not yet seem to have found the Hall of Justice; it looked just the same as it had looked for all Ven's life, the same as it had looked for all the nine hundred years that there had been people in the Heligan Structure. There was the seat where the Justiciar would sit, the benches for the observers, the dock where the Doctor would stand, and behind that, towering over everything, the great statue, which the founders had carved so that their descendants would never forget their ancient enemy.

'Who's that supposed to be?' asked the Doctor, glancing up at it.

'That is you,' said the Justiciar, but she sounded uncertain. She looked from the face of the Doctor to the face of the carving, trying to detect a similarity. She said, 'That is how the Doctor appeared to our ancestors, nine hundred years ago.'

'It looks nothing like him!' said Leela.

'Oh, I don't know,' said the Doctor. 'There is a certain resemblance. Two eyes, two ears, one nose – I suppose you could call that a nose? – and it's true that I've changed a bit over the years. But I'm certain I've never looked like that.'

'He's so young!' said Leela. 'And so handsome!'

'I mean, he's wearing a bow tie!' the Doctor

explained patiently. 'Ridiculous objects! I wouldn't be seen dead in a bow tie!'

'The Doctor told our ancestors "Bow ties are cool",' said Ven.

'Cool?' The Doctor blinked at him. 'I would never have said . . . Oh, wait! Hang on! Ah! I think I see what's happened. That fellow must be one of my *future* regenerations. These things you blame me for, the revolt of the Thara, your exile from Golrandonvar . . . they haven't happened yet. Not for me. And you can't hold me responsible for something I haven't done yet. Would that be justice, Justiciar?'

'I suppose not . . .'

'We should kill him anyway!' said one of Ratisbon's men. 'Then he will never be able to betray our ancestors and help the Thara.'

'No,' said the Doctor, 'that wouldn't do any good. If you kill me now I won't be able to visit Golrandonvar, the Thara may never revolt, this

Heligan will never exist and you won't be here to kill me. You would all vanish instantly in a puff of paradoxes.'

Another great quake shook the hall; shook the whole wooden city. Carved panels dropped from the roof. The statue of the future Doctor swayed drunkenly.

'This tree is angry,' blurted Leela.

'You're right,' the Doctor said.

'Am I?' She blinked at him. 'Are you not going to say that I am being unscientific?'

'These tree-quakes, the way the spores are behaving . . .' said the Doctor. 'Justiciar, I don't think your founders were being honest with you. Your Director Sprawn didn't really trust his descendants to bring me to justice. He knew he couldn't rely on you to stay angry all those years. He knew you'd grow too reasonable, too merciful. He just needed you to keep the tree alive. To do a bit of light pruning and keep an eye out for greenfly until I returned. Then it would take its own revenge. Even if that means destroying itself – and all of you.'

There were moans and cries of woe from his listeners. 'What can we do?' asked the Justiciar.

The Doctor smiled that wide, delighted smile of his. 'Oh, we'll think of something! Now, an organism as complex as a Heligan, especially one this big, must be controlled from somewhere. There must be a central brain of some sort, which sensed the arrival of the TARDIS and triggered the release of those spores.'

'The root ball?' suggested Ven. 'It's down in the Heartwood, beneath the digestion chamber, at the very centre of the tree.'

'Can you show me the way?'

Ven looked at his mother, then back at the Doctor. He nodded.

'I am coming with you!' Leela said.

'No, Leela, you stay here; they'll need you if

the spores attack. Don't worry; I'll be back in two ticks!'

'Doctor . . .!'

But he was already gone, loping after Ven to a small door on the far side of the hall and vanishing through it into shadows.

Leela turned to the others. 'How long is a tick?' she asked. But they didn't know, and hadn't time to answer anyway. The Hall of Justice was suddenly full of the sound of spore-roots battering against the doors.

'It is forbidden to go any further,' he warned, peering down the last passage that led into the root ball. Cobwebs hung like curtains, stirring softly in a wind that seemed to come from the heart of the tree. A faint, silvery light showed at the far end.

'Oh well, rules are made to be broken!' said the Doctor cheerfully, and then, seeing how afraid the boy was, added, 'All right, you stay here. Shout if any of those spores come poking about, eh?'

He went on alone, using his hat to sweep aside the cobwebs. The light grew brighter. He emerged into a space whose walls and floor and roof were made of ancient, interwoven roots. Tangled among the roots was machinery torn from the guts of an old starship; one of those twenty-fourth-century computers with the big dials and buttons, controlling the flow of chemicals through the Heligan's boughs. Wires and coloured flexes led from the machines, wrapped around the roots like strands of ivy leading up into the ceiling. The

Doctor followed them, looking up into the shadows above his head.

Among the twistings and knottings of the wood, two eyes were watching him.

'Ah!' said the Doctor. 'Director Sprawn, I presume?'

He could make out a face around the eyes now, ancient, mutated, scarcely human, sprouting twigs and tendrils like a carving of the Green Man in a country church. There were the suggestions of a body, spreadeagled on the ceiling, almost engulfed in the web of roots. So that was how Sprawn had made sure the Heligan would do his bidding, even after all these years. He had become a part of it.

They barred the doors, but the spores burst through them. They piled up benches, but the spores shoved those easily aside. And then it was all fright and confusion and the hack and thrust of spears, the screams of the people snatched by the spores, the shouts of their comrades as they fought to tear them free, the squeals of children hiding behind their mothers at the far side of the hall. And Aggie and Leela sap-spattered, fighting side by side, spear and knife and desperate courage against the spines and tendrils of the spores . . .

'So, Doctor!' growled the face in the ceiling, root-muffled. 'We meet again!'

'Well, we're meeting for the first time, technically, Sprawn,' said the Doctor, looking quickly around at the machinery. 'Though we *will* meet again, nine hundred years in the past. Your past: my future. That's the trouble with time travel, you never know whether you're coming or going . . .'

He reached over and turned one of the knobs on the nearest control panel. It seemed to do nothing but draw an angry hiss from the face above him.

'The Heligan will tear itself apart rather than let

you escape, Doctor! We shall be avenged at last for what you did to us all those centuries ago!'

The Doctor nibbled a fingernail, his eyes still on the controls. Absent-mindedly he said, 'Ah yes, about that. I can just about accept that I might, one day, in a moment of weakness, wear a bow tie, but there is no way I will ever take up arms against anyone unless they thoroughly deserve it. I don't think you and your fellow colonists on Golrandonvar were innocent victims of the Thara rebellion at all. I think you were vicious tyrants.'

'The Thara were vermin!' shouted the face in the ceiling. 'They opposed every improvement we tried to make to their benighted world!'

'Improvements like altering their atmosphere?'

'Golrandonvar had to be terraformed: turned into a world fit for people, not those methane-breathing swamp-monkeys. We had no choice but to exterminate them!'

'Now that's a word I've never liked,' said the

Doctor, starting to sound quite stern. 'I can see why my future self is going to help them to get rid of you. Just as I'm going to have to help your own people now, to save them from your suicidal rage.'

'Let them die!' screamed the mad face above him. 'What have they to live for? For nine hundred years they've scraped a living in this wretched weed, imprisoned by your moralistic meddling!'

'Wretched?' asked the Doctor. He tried another dial, and chuckled delightedly when it produced a beeping noise and a bubbling of amber fluid in a glass container buried deep among the roots. 'Oh, I think they've done rather well with the place, all things considered. They're ready to move on. Except you didn't exactly play fair with them, did you? This tree should have had offspring, a forest of Heligans that would have made the world below us habitable. But you didn't want that. If they'd had a new world to build, your descendants might have forgotten all about their vengeance. So you made some changes to the genome, didn't you? Stopped the Heligan producing spores at all, until now . . .'

'Doctor!' There were scrabbling sounds from the passage outside. Ven came hurrying in, bearded with cobwebs, still scared of the forbidden chamber, but more scared of what was outside it. 'There are spores coming!'

'I have called them here to kill you, Doctor,' said the head in the ceiling, and it began to laugh. Saliva pattered on the brim of the Doctor's hat.

'And that's another thing,' the Doctor said, while his hands went spidering over the controls and the machinery beeped and burped. 'Heligan spores aren't normally aggressive. You must have tampered with the chemical messages that control their behaviour . . .'

'Doctor!' Ven fled to the far end of the chamber as the first spore came pushing its way along the passage, reaching out with woody limbs.

'It's all right, Ven,' said the Doctor. 'The only

things that Heligan spores naturally attack are parasites that threaten their parent tree. Now I've adjusted the chemical balance, they should start to behave normally again . . .'

The spore reached past the Doctor. Its tendrils took hold of the roots that formed the wall. It climbed awkwardly, like a land crab. Other spores entered, and also started climbing. The thing that had been Director Sprawn watched, wide-eyed. He tried to struggle free of the ceiling, but his limbs were roots, his flesh was wood, the stuff of the tree was woven through him. He shrieked as the spores clustered around him. Stone-hard root-tips rose and fell like axes, hacking and hewing, splattering thick sap. The shrieks did not last long.

'What are they doing to him?' asked Ven.

'He's being pruned,' said the Doctor. 'Cut out . . .' He felt sorry for Sprawn. In many ways it was a wonderful achievement, this great tree that he'd created. If only he had been able to enjoy it for what it was, instead of poisoning it with his need for vengeance.

'Will the Heligan be all right without him?' asked Ven.

'Oh, I should think so,' said the Doctor.

Some of the spores had now turned their attention to the machinery, driving their roots through the old computer casings, ripping out spaghetti-tangles of electronic innards in fountains of dazzling sparks. Blinking away the after-images of the explosions, the Doctor started to lead Ven back up the passageway towards the outer branches and the others.

'In fact,' he said, 'I should think it will be a great deal better off . . .'

In the Hall of Justice the spores had stopped attacking all at once, suddenly going still, as if they had forgotten what they were supposed to be doing – or remembered.

'It's the Doctor!' said Leela, wiping the sap from her knife as she turned to the others. 'He's done it!'

Her comrades were not so sure. They watched warily, holding their spears ready. When the spores all suddenly shuffled into life again a few moments later, they leaped hastily back behind their barricades of piled-up benches.

But the spores were not returning to the attack. Ignoring the humans, they rustled their way to the hall's huge, misty windows. The cellulose tore as they leaned their spiny shapes hard against it. They clustered on the windowsills, tensing their many legs, and then, one by one, they sprang out, releasing jets of pent-up gas to help thrust themselves free of the Heligan's gravity.

'There!' said the Doctor, sauntering in with his hands in his pockets, Ven close behind him. 'Look at that! Another ten years or so and that world we're orbiting should start to be quite habitable.'

'Ten years, Doctor?' The Justiciar turned to look

at him. She still felt faintly that she was failing in her duty by not making him stand trial, but so much had happened since his arrival, so much had changed . . . 'What shall we do in the meantime?' she asked.

'Oh, you should branch out!' the Doctor said with a grin. 'Think about advertising this place. A tree of this size, surrounded by its own floating forest – it must be one of the wonders of the galaxy! You should try luring tourists instead of Time Lords . . .'

From every window of the Heligan Structure now the spores were taking flight, unfurling their first young branches as they spread across the sky. The humans stood wonderstruck, gazing at the airborne forest that they had seeded. Ven took Aggie's hand. The Doctor tapped Leela on the shoulder and nodded towards the door.

★

'So,' the Doctor asked, a while later, when they had managed to cut a way through the woody stems to the door of the TARDIS. 'Seen enough trees for a bit?'

'I do not care if I never see another,' said Leela.

'Excellent! Because I was thinking the sand-reefs of Phenostris IV might be worth a look. I haven't been there since . . .'

The door closed behind them. After a few moments, the TARDIS slowly dematerialised, leaving a TARDIS-shaped cage of branches to mark the place where it had stood. The noise of its going echoed and re-echoed through the passageways and chambers of the Heartwood, but there was nobody to hear it. All the people of the Heligan Structure were crowding at its windows, watching as the skies of the world below them filled with newborn trees.

About the Author

Philip Reeve was born in Brighton and worked in a bookshop for many years before becoming a full-time illustrator and then turning to writing.

His first novel, *Mortal Engines*, won the Nestlé Smarties Gold Award (2002), the Blue Peter Book of the Year Award, and was shortlisted for both the Branford Boase Award and the Whitbread Children's Book Award. He has since won many more awards and accolades for his works including the Guardian Children's Fiction Prize in 2006 and the Los Angeles Times Book Award for *A Darkling*

Plain and the 2008 CILIP Carnegie Medal for *Here Lies Arthur*. His most recent titles are *GOBLINS* (2012), which was shortlisted for the Roald Dahl Funny Prize and its sequel *GOBLINS VS DWARVES* (2013).

He lives in Dartmoor, England, with his wife and son, Sam. For further information and to explore the author's own curious world visit www.philip-reeve.com

BBC

DOCTOR WHO

HOLLY BLACK
NEIL GAIMAN
DEREK LANDY
CHARLIE HIGSON
ALEX SCARROW
MALORIE BLACKMAN
RICHELLE MEAD
PATRICK NESS
PHILIP REEVE
MARCUS SEDGWICK
MICHAEL SCOTT
EOIN COLFER

12 DOCTORS 12 STORIES

Available in
Puffin Audio

Scan the QR code to listen to an extract from the audiobook
edition of *Doctor Who: 12 Doctors 12 Stories*.

http://snd.sc/1hw8FQy

It all started with a Scarecrow

Puffin is over seventy years old.
Sounds ancient, doesn't it? But Puffin has never been
so lively. We're always on the lookout for the next big
idea, which is how it began all those years ago.

Penguin Books was a big idea from the mind of
a man called Allen Lane, who in 1935 invented
the quality paperback and changed the world.
**And from great Penguins, great Puffins grew,
changing the face of children's books forever.**

The first four Puffin Picture Books were hatched in 1940 and the
first Puffin story book featured a man with broomstick arms called
Worzel Gummidge. In 1967 Kaye Webb, Puffin Editor, started the
Puffin Club, promising to **'make children into readers'**.
She kept that promise and over 200,000 children became devoted
Puffineers through their quarterly instalments of *Puffin Post*.

Many years from now, we hope you'll look back and
remember Puffin with a smile. **No matter what your age
or what you're into, there's a Puffin for everyone.**
The possibilities are endless, but one thing is for sure:
whether it's a picture book or a paperback, a sticker book
or a hardback, **if it's got that little Puffin
on it – it's bound to be good.**

YOUR STORY
STARTS HERE

Do you **love books** and
discovering new stories?
Then **www.puffinbooks.com** is the
place for you . . .

- Thrilling adventures, fantastic fiction
  and laugh-out-loud fun

- Brilliant videos featuring your favourite authors
  and characters

- Exciting competitions, news, activities,
  the Puffin blog and SO MUCH more . . .

www.puffinbooks.com